Ladybird books are widely available, but in case of
difficulty may be ordered by post or telephone from:

Ladybird Books – Cash Sales Department
Littlegate Road Paignton Devon TQ3 3BE
Telephone 01803 554761

A catalogue record for this book is available
from the British Library

Published by Ladybird Books Ltd Loughborough Leicestershire UK
Ladybird Books Ltd is a subsidiary of the Penguin Group of companies
LADYBIRD and the device of a Ladybird are trademarks of Ladybird Books Ltd

One summer's day, Alice and her
kitten, Dinah, were sitting in the
branches of a tree. Down below,
her sister was reading aloud from
a history book.

But Alice wasn't listening. She was dreaming of a world where cats and rabbits wore clothes and lived in little houses. She picked up Dinah and climbed down from the tree.

Just then, a white rabbit came scuttling along. He was clutching a large watch.

The White Rabbit looked at his
watch as he ran past Alice, muttering,
"I'm late! I'm late!"

"How curious," gasped Alice. "What
could a rabbit possibly be late for?
Please!" she cried. "Wait for me."

But the rabbit didn't stop. "I'm late! I'm late!" he cried and disappeared into a large hole at the foot of a tree.

Alice was now *very* curious. She squeezed into the dark hole and crawled after him.

Suddenly, Alice found herself falling down, down, down. Luckily, her dress ballooned out like a parachute and she began floating. Hanging on the walls of the tunnel were all kinds of strange pictures and furniture.

At last, Alice reached the bottom. The White Rabbit was just disappearing round a corner at the end of a very long corridor.

"Wait!" cried Alice, chasing after him.

At the end of the corridor was a tiny door. Alice tried the doorknob.

"Eek!" cried a voice – the doorknob was speaking!

"I'm looking for the White Rabbit," said Alice. "Please let me through."

"Sorry! You're *much* too big," replied the doorknob. "Try the bottle on the table over there."

Alice looked round and saw the bottle labelled – *drink me*.

Alice tasted a little. Soon, she had finished *every* drop.

All at once, Alice began to shrink! Soon, she was so tiny that she was able to get through the little door.

On the other side of the door, Alice
found herself on the edge of a large
forest. She saw the White Rabbit
through the trees in the distance.
Alice started to run after him, but
suddenly her way was blocked by
two little fat men – Tweedle Dum
and Tweedle Dee.

"My name is Alice," said Alice.
"I'm curious to know where the
White Rabbit is going."

The two little men both began talking
at the same time. Alice couldn't
understand what they were saying,
so she decided to set off in another
direction.

Soon, Alice came to a little house. As she walked up the path, the White Rabbit ran out of the front door. He was now dressed in a tunic and a ruff.

"Oh, my! I'm late! I'm late!" he cried. Then he said to Alice, "Go and get my gloves!"

Alice was too surprised to argue and went inside the little house.

Alice searched *everywhere*.

Finally, she lifted the lid of a jar and found some biscuits. They looked very good to eat, so she took one...

Alice started to grow, and grow, and grow! Soon, she was so big that she was bursting out of the house! Her arms poked through the windows and her legs burst out of the door.

"A monster!" cried the White Rabbit.

"Perhaps if I find something else to eat," said Alice, "it will make me small again." She stretched out her hand and pulled up a carrot from the garden. When Alice ate it, she began to shrink!

Soon, Alice was so small she could crawl *under* the front door. The rabbit, pleased that the monster had disappeared, ran off down the garden.

Alice tried to follow him. But now that she was so tiny, the grass seemed like a *huge* forest.

"And who are you?" asked a sleepy voice. It was a caterpillar, lying lazily on a mushroom.

"I'm Alice," replied Alice. "And I wish I was a little taller."

Suddenly, the caterpillar turned into a butterfly. "I can help," said the butterfly, pointing at the mushroom. "One side of this will make you taller, the other side will make you shorter." Then, the butterfly fluttered away.

Alice looked at the mushroom, trying to decide which side would make her taller. Finally, she broke off a piece from each side and took a large bite from one.

Luckily, Alice had chosen the correct piece and was soon back to her normal height. She dropped the pieces of mushroom into her pocket.

Walking along, Alice heard singing. She turned to see a toothy smile and a pair of eyes.

As Alice looked more closely, an odd-looking cat with purple stripes appeared.

"I'm looking for the White Rabbit," said Alice. "Which way should I go?"

23

"I'm the Cheshire Cat," said the odd-looking cat. "And if *I* was looking for a White Rabbit I'd ask the Mad Hatter or the March Hare. That way." And he pointed towards a path in the forest. Then, the Cheshire Cat vanished.

So, Alice followed the path and soon heard the Mad Hatter and the March Hare singing. They were having tea at a big table set with many places.

"We're having an un-birthday party,"
said the Mad Hatter. "We have one
birthday a year, so there are three
hundred and sixty-four un-birthdays!"

The March Hare asked Alice where she had come from.

"It all started while I was sitting with Dinah, my cat..." began Alice.

"Cat?" said a squeaky voice. A dormouse jumped out of a teapot and ran around the table.

"Catch him!" called the Mad Hatter.

"No time! No time! I'm late!" cried
the White Rabbit, magically
appearing. But once again, he
disappeared into the distance.

"Wait!" shouted Alice, getting up
from the table and following him.

By now, Alice was tired of the strange ways of Wonderland. "I'm going home," she said.

"You can't go home without meeting the Queen," said the Cheshire Cat, suddenly appearing. As he spoke, a door in a nearby tree opened. Stepping through it, Alice found herself in the palace gardens. She was amazed to see two playing cards painting white roses with red paint!

The cards explained that the Queen of Hearts had ordered red roses. They were painting the white roses red in the hope that she wouldn't notice. If the Queen did notice the white roses, she would chop off their heads!

Just then, the doors of the palace opened and out marched the White Rabbit.

"The Queen of Hearts," he announced, "and the King."

The Queen walked up to the rose tree. "Who's been painting my roses red?" she demanded. "Off with their heads!" Then she spotted Alice.

Alice trembled. "I'm trying to find my way home," she said.

"Your way?" cried the Queen. "*All* the ways here belong to *me*! Off with her head!"

Then the Queen changed her mind. "Do you play croquet?" she asked.

"Yes, Your Majesty," replied Alice.

"Then let the game begin," ordered the Queen.

Alice had never seen such a curious croquet game before. The balls were hedgehogs and the mallets were flamingos!

As the Queen was about to take a shot with her flamingo, the Cheshire Cat appeared. The Queen's flamingo panicked. In the confusion, the Queen lost her balance and fell over. She was furious. "Off with her head!" she yelled at Alice.

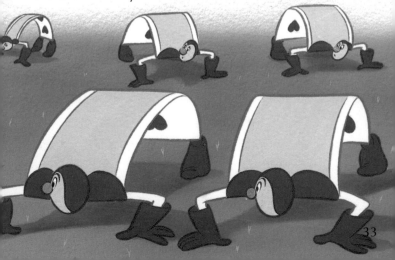

"Shouldn't she have a trial first?"
said the King.

"Very well," sighed the Queen.

So, everyone went to the courtroom
and Alice was put on trial. The
Queen sat on the judge's bench.

"The prisoner is accused of tricking
Her Majesty into a game of croquet,"
said the White Rabbit.

"Never mind all that!" the Queen shouted. "Guilty! Off with her head!"

"Shouldn't we call some witnesses?" asked the King.

"Very well!" the Queen snapped. "But get on with it."

35

The first witness was the March Hare. Then came the dormouse, followed by the Mad Hatter.

At that moment, the Cheshire Cat appeared. "Look, Your Majesty," said Alice. "The Cheshire Cat."

Immediately, the dormouse jumped
out of his teapot. He ran up and
down the courtroom squeaking.
Everyone chased after him.

Then, Alice remembered the pieces of mushroom in her pocket and took a bite from one. She started growing and growing. Everyone was terrified.

"Off with her..." but before the Queen could finish, Alice said, "You don't frighten me. You're just a bad-tempered old Queen!"

No sooner had Alice spoken than she felt herself shrinking again.

"Now, what were you saying, my dear?" asked the Queen.

Alice fled from the courtroom.

She was soon lost in a maze of hedges.
She could still hear the Queen's voice
but it sounded very far away now –
as if in a dream.

All of a sudden, she heard someone
calling her. "Alice, please wake up!"
It was her sister. "You've been asleep
for a *very* long time. Can you remember
anything from your history lesson?"

Alice rubbed her eyes. Dinah was curled up in her lap, fast asleep.

"I've had such an exciting time," said Alice. "There was a White Rabbit and I followed him and…"

"Oh, never mind," said Alice's sister. "It's time to go home for tea."

Alice picked up her kitten. "You know, Dinah," she said, "maybe I'll stay in the real world after all."